the end

D06338 61

Then Mom's voice whispered
"Don't worry, it's just me.
When I said 'Goodnight' just now,
I forgot to give you this."

Then Monster Mom gave Oakey
a goodnight kiss!

The monster leaned over him and Oakey closed his eyes. What happened next gave Oakey an enormous surprise. The monster picked him up and cuddled him tight. Monsters just don't do that.

This couldn't be right!

And then Oakey saw it,
standing by the door.
The monster!

It moved across the floor and
walked straight towards him,
with its arms stretched out.
Oakey's mouth opened,
but he found he couldn't shout.

"They're just your slippers, Oakey, so there's no need to hide. They won't be creeping anywhere without your feet inside," grinned Mom. "That's it now, Oakey. Time to say goodnight."

Mom turned and left the room, switching off the light.

"Why aren't you asleep?"
asked Mom.

"There are
huge creepy crawlies
underneath my bed.
And I can't get the thought of them
out of my head,"
complained Oakey.

Oakey's ears drooped
and he got into bed.
But he didn't
close his eyes.

"Oh, Oakey, you've made a mistake.
The only thing underneath the sheets,
is your old teddy bear," smiled Mom.

"Why aren't you in bed, Oakey?"
asked Mom.

"There's a
great big lump
beneath the sheets.
It's waiting to get me.
I'm scared it's going to pounce.
Please come and see,"
sniffed Oakey.

Oakey's ears drooped and
off he went.
But he was
back in a flash!

"Oh, Oakey, you've made a mistake.
That's no ghost.
It's just an old coat, hanging on the hook.
Coats don't float!" laughed Mom.

"What's the matter?"
asked Mom.

"There's a ghost
in the hallway, hovering around.
Look, there it is floating
just above the ground,"
he wailed.

Oakey's ears drooped
and off he went.
But he was
back in a flash!

Mom laughed.
"Oh, Oakey, you've made
a mistake.
That's no monster. It's a mop."
And she gave the mop a shake.

"Where's your drink?" asked Mom.
"You haven't been very long.
You look scared, Oakey.
Is there something wrong?"

"There's a monster
in the kitchen,
with long, white shaggy hair,
lurking in the corner,
behind the rocking chair,"
said Oakey.

Oakey's ears drooped and off he went.
But he was **back in a flash!**

"Have a drink first," smiled Mom, "then you must go."

"Five minutes more!" begged Oakey.

Mom answered, "No!"

Oakey curled up in the chair.
His ears began to droop and he muttered,
"Oh, that's not fair!"

"It's bedtime now,
Oakey," said Mom.

Goodnight kiss

Written by Jillian Harker
Illustrated by Andrew-Everitt-Stewart

p